Welcome to the world of Beast Quest!

Tom was once an ordinary village boy, until he travelled to the City, met King Hugo and discovered his destiny. Now he is the Master of the Beasts, sworn to defend Avantia and its people against Evil. Tom draws on the might of the magical Golden Armour, and is protected by powerful tokens granted to him by the Good Beasts of Avantia. Tom and his loyal companion Elenna are always ready to visit new lands and tackle the enemies of the realm.

While there's blood in his veins, Tom will never give up the Quest…

BLOOD VALLEY

FROZEN LAKE

There are special gold coins to
collect in this book. You will earn
one coin for every chapter you read.

Find out what to do with your coins
at the end of the book.

CONTENTS

It's been many years since I crossed the borders of Avantia. I can't say I've missed the place much. Last time I was here, my plan to conquer the kingdom was foiled by a mere boy, though he calls himself their Master of the Beasts.

Now I serve a new and cruel master. Though he looks like a man, he has the cold heart of a monster. We have travelled day and night from the Wildlands north of Avantia's frozen wastes, and at last the walls of the City loom into view.

I have heard the boy Tom is still alive. I wonder what he will think when he sees me again. And I wonder if he will understand the terrible danger that is about to be unleashed.

One thing is certain – the kingdom and its people are going to suffer a terrible fate.

Yours,

Kapra the Witch

SIGHTMIST

Tom stared into the broken tomb. The last sliver of sun had fallen below the horizon, draining all colour from the barren Wildlands. A sudden gust of wind tore through his clothes, making him shiver. Inside the stone sarcophagus, the bones of a corpse poked from a suit of rusted armour. Even if the flesh had long since decomposed, there could be no doubt who it was. The grime-encrusted gold ring on one of the skeleton's fingers had belonged to King Theo, who had given it to his eldest son Angelo, more than thirty years ago. At Tom's side, Elenna let out a heavy sigh.

"What a sad end for a brave man," she said. "An unmarked grave in a foreign land..."

Tom bowed his head. "Yes. But at least now we know we were right. The real Angelo lies here, which means the tyrant currently sitting on Hugo's throne is an imposter, and not his brother at all. But how can that be?"

The age-worn shaman who had led them to the grave shook his head, his bone necklaces clacking together. "All I know is that the Avantian warrior who led his forces against our people lies here," he said.

At the sound of footsteps, Tom looked up. Even in the failing light, he recognised the tall, muscular girl striding towards them as Lika, the brave daughter of a barbarian clan leader who had helped Tom and Elenna discover the truth about Angelo. As Lika's eyes fell on the shaman, she scowled. The holy man had helped his own clan's leader, Jax, control a Beast called

Krotax, using it to terrorise Lika's people. She had been injured during Tom and Elenna's recent fight to defeat Krotax, and now her arm was in a sling. As Lika drew near to the grave, her eyes widened.

"A body?" she asked, making a hand gesture as if to ward off evil.

Tom nodded. "It's Angelo," he said. "He still wears his father's ring." Ignoring the creeping feeling running over his skin, Tom bent to prise the ring from the skeleton's finger.

Lika gasped, shocked. "What are you doing?"

Tom slipped the ring into his

pocket and brushed the clinging
grave dust from his hands, trying
not to shudder.

"This ring will prove we have
seen Angelo's body when we reach
Avantia," Tom said. "Now we have it,

we must return home."

Elenna shook her head, frowning. "We can't just charge back into the palace and declare Angelo a fraud," she said. "His soldiers will be out looking for us. I doubt we'll even get within arrowshot of the City before we're caught."

Tom's shoulders sagged. The terrible feeling of dread and hopelessness that he had carried ever since the evil witch Kapra had stripped him of his powers on Angelo's orders weighed him down more heavily than ever. *Without my Golden Armour, and magical jewels and tokens, how can I hope to face Angelo's army...?* Tom gritted his teeth and forced himself to stand tall. "Maybe you're right," he told Elenna. "But we have to try, at least! What choice do we have?"

"There is one other way to get word to your home kingdom," Lika said. She turned to look pointedly at the shaman, one eyebrow raised.

"No!" the old man said, holding up his gnarled hands. "That is not a good idea. Not a good idea at all."

"What isn't?" Tom asked.

"Here in the Wildlands, there is a thing called Sightmist," Lika said. "It's a magical vapour that allows a person to see and even speak with someone far away. Being a man of magic, he should be able to make it," she added, jabbing a thumb towards the shaman.

"You don't know what you're talking about!" the old man snapped. Then his voice took on a whiny note. "It takes time to make Sightmist. I haven't done it for years. And what if it goes wrong? The results could be disastrous."

"We're willing to take that risk," Tom said. "A kingdom is at stake, and really, we have no other choice."

"What if *I'm* not willing to risk it?" the shaman said.

Lika fixed the old man with a steady gaze. "What if I decide I'm not willing to risk keeping you around after you tried to feed me to a Beast?" she said.

The shaman twisted his hands together, scowling. "Fine!" he said at last. "Make a small fire. I will prepare the spell."

"We should cover Angelo's grave first," Elenna said.

Tom nodded. "I'll do that. You and Lika gather kindling."

As Tom took one last look at Angelo's body, pity and sorrow swelled inside him for the young warrior buried so far from home. *I will not rest until all of Avantia knows the truth!* Tom vowed. Then he pulled the sarcophagus lid closed and began to pile stones back over the tomb.

Before long, Angelo's skeleton lay buried once more beneath its unmarked cairn, and a small blaze crackled nearby. Elenna blew into the fire, making it flare up, then fed a handful of twigs into the flames.

Tom glanced towards the old shaman sitting on a rock a little way off with his chin on his chest.

"Shouldn't you be putting together some ingredients or something?" Tom asked.

The shaman started as if he'd been half asleep, then shrugged. "I'm ready when you are. All I need is an object from the place you want to visit. Do you have anything from your city with you?"

"I've got my arrowheads," Elenna said. "They were forged in the City. Will they do?"

The shaman nodded. He rose slowly and shuffled over to the fire, where Elenna handed him one of her arrows. Tom and Lika joined them. As the flames popped and cracked, sending glowing sparks up into the gloom, the shaman lifted the arrow to his lips. He chanted a few strange words, then, with a gruff cry, thrust the arrow's metal tip deep into the heart of the blaze.

The shaman's body started to shake as he held the arrow in the fire. His eyes rolled back and he grimaced, his feathered headdress trembling in time with his juddering body. Finally, he let out a ragged cry and lifted the arrow from the flames. Thick grey smoke poured from the heated metal tip.

Moving the arrow from side to side, with long, sweeping strokes, the old man traced the shape of a door in the air. The smoke hung like fog, creating a wall of grey vapour, swirling and writhing before them.

"It is done!" the shaman said hoarsely. He lowered the arrow, breathing heavily, then hobbled away from the flames.

Lika turned to Tom and Elenna, her brows pinched together with worry. "Now you must step into the mist," she told them. "Picture the place you wish to see in your mind. When you reach your destination, you will be invisible. To speak with anyone, you will need to get very close. But be careful. If your mind wanders, there is no knowing where you will end up, or whether you will return."

Tom and Elenna exchanged uneasy glances, then they each took a steadying breath. "Focus on the City," Tom told Elenna. "Head for the gate. We can start our search from there."

Elenna nodded. Tom took her hand. Then together they stepped into the mist...

A VISION OF HOME

Tom felt the ground beneath him
drop away, but before he could fall,
a strong wind snatched him up,
dragging his legs out behind him.
He gripped Elenna's hand tightly
as smoke streamed past…or was
it cloud? The swirling greyness
below him parted, and he caught a
glimpse of dark forest speeding by…

mountains…the snaking shape of a
river, silver with reflected moonlight.
I have to focus on the City! he told
himself. Trying to ignore the dizzying
sense of speed, he forced himself to
visualise the main gates.

Dark plains of rolling grassland
whooshed by, half hidden by the

billowing greyness. Tom spotted
flickering orange points of light
ahead which quickly became
burning torches set on high stone
walls... *The City!* But as the outer
walls drew closer, Tom felt his
stomach twist with dread. The flags
and banners that usually welcomed

visitors had gone. Instead, scores
of soldiers topped the battlements,
wielding bows and spears. They
scowled as they gazed out over the
kingdom, pacing up and down like
caged dogs hungry for a fight.

Tom gasped as a sudden thrust
of speed sent him swooping over
the city walls. He and Elenna sped
down familiar streets where now
the doors and windows had been
shuttered and barred. Pairs of armed
soldiers stood at every corner, and
grey-faced citizens scurried by, their
faces etched with fear. Tom and
Elenna rushed past taverns where
harsh voices rang into the night, and
through deserted market squares

that should have been busy with evening traders. Burning fury seared through Tom's veins. *What has the imposter king done to my home?*

"We should head to the palace," he told Elenna.

"But Daltec will be in hiding," Elenna reminded him.

Frustration burned in Tom's chest. "Then he could be anywhere!" he said.

"No," Elenna said. "Daltec promised to keep an eye on Angelo and his witch Kapra, which means he must be close."

More dark and half-deserted streets rushed by. The guttering flames of lamps made the shadows dance like evil spirits. "There!" Elenna said, pointing into a narrow alleyway to their left.

Tom spotted a tall, slender figure with a familiar hesitant stride hurrying towards them. A dirty cloak hung from his shoulders, but Tom recognised the angular features and dark eyes of his friend immediately. *Daltec!*

All at once, the swooping, whooshing sensation stopped, and Tom felt his feet touch the cobbles. The sudden stillness made his head spin and he almost stumbled. Daltec strode on towards them, his head bowed, muttering something under his breath.

"Daltec!" Tom said, stepping out
into the young wizard's path. Daltec
leaped back, his eyes wide with fear.

"It's Tom and Elenna," Tom said.
"But you can't see us."

"Where are you?" Daltec hissed,

staring about wildly.

"We're still in the Wildlands," Elenna said. "But a shaman cast a spell to allow us to speak with you."

"Wait," Daltec said. He glanced warily up and down the alleyway, then ducked inside a shadow alcove and beckoned for them to follow.

"All right," Daltec said, swallowing hard. "We should be safe here for a moment. Are you both well?"

"Yes," Tom said, "and we have discovered the truth. As the legends told, the real Angelo died in battle long ago. I've seen his body and I have King Theo's ring, taken from his grave. The man that now holds

Hugo's throne is not his brother. Send word to Aduro and Hugo in Tangala – the king must return and reclaim his crown before the kingdom and its people suffer more injustice."

Daltec frowned. "It will take time for the message to reach Hugo," he said.

"Then send it at once," Tom said. "We will return to the City as quickly as we can, and challenge the fake Angelo. But alone and without my powers, I fear we cannot win. We will need Hugo and any forces he can muster."

"Who are you talking to?" a harsh voice growled. Tom spun to see a huge soldier with furious, bloodshot eyes under thick black brows staring right through him, at Daltec.

"I...er..." Daltec started, but Tom didn't hear anything else. Clouds of smoke billowed up before him, hiding the soldier's face. The smoke filled Tom's lungs, making him cough and his eyes stream. He waved it away with his hand and blinked, to find himself standing before the campfire beside Elenna, under the wide, starry sky of the Wildlands.

1

THE FROZEN FIELDS

As the last curling tendrils of smoke wafted away, Tom saw Lika grinning with relief. "You're back!" she cried.

Tom nodded. "But now we need to reach Avantia more urgently than ever. What is the quickest way?"

Lika's smile faded and she looked uneasy. "The ice pass is by far the shortest route," she said, "but at this time of year it's treacherous. There are glacial lakes in the mountains, and the ice won't be thick yet – you would be better off taking the longer route through the marshes. Perhaps four days, or five."

"We don't have time," Tom said. "We'll have to take our chances in the mountains."

Lika nodded. "Then eat first. We'll lend you cloaks. But you will need to be very careful. A creature lives among the lakes. I've never seen it, but each year we hear of livestock being taken by a Beast – even the odd traveller."

Tom felt a pang of fear, but clenched his fists.

"That tyrant who calls himself Angelo destroyed my armour, and he's destroying the City," he said, glancing at Elenna. "While there is blood in my veins, I'll stop him!"

After a quick meal of bread and stew, Tom and Elenna said their goodbyes to Lika and her clan. The landscape looked silver-grey in the moonlight as they set off along a winding footpath that led between outcrops of barren rock.

As the moon travelled higher into the cloudless sky, Tom and Elenna found their way steepening before them. The coarse grass petered out, until only pale lichen and stunted bushes clung to the jagged rocks that fringed their path. An icy wind whipped tears into Tom's eyes, and he drew his cloak tighter about himself.

Tom and Elenna climbed higher, their footsteps ringing in the cold, thin air. As they gained height, a glittering frost covered the ground and their breath hung in frozen puffs before them. Glancing back, Tom could see the barren Wildlands spread far below, shrouded in darkness. Ahead, ice-frosted rock gleamed in the moonlight. Thick, compacted snow crunched beneath their boots, and ice dunes rippled away into the hazy distance.

Suddenly, Elenna stopped and held up her hand. Tom fell still at her side, listening. The distant clatter of hoofbeats echoed from above them, getting closer by the moment.

Tom tensed, his hand on the hilt of his sword.

"A Beast?" Elenna said.

But Tom shook his head. "There are too many hoofbeats. Maybe mounted soldiers?" He glanced about, looking for somewhere to hide, but before he could move, a herd of shaggy cattle crested the rise ahead of them, snorting and puffing in the cold air. Among the

woolly animals, Tom made out the
unmistakable shapes of several tall
men clad in furs. He felt a burning
knot of frustration rise in his chest.

Normally, he would greet the men, and ask for news, knowing that with his powers he could hold his own if things turned nasty. But now he couldn't take that risk. *I have to get to Avantia, and fast.*

"This way," Tom told Elenna, slipping down from the path to climb among the jagged rocks. They crept along a perilous ledge with a flat plain of glittering white spread below them. A frozen lake, Tom realised. Suddenly, a deep horn blast sounded from somewhere nearby. Tom's pulse quickened as the clatter of hoofbeats became frenzied, mingled with urgent shouts. Tom felt the rock shake beneath his feet as the charging herd drew close.

"We need to get lower or we'll be seen," Elenna said, easing herself from the ledge on to the ice below. Tom followed her, then they both dropped down on to the pale surface of the frozen lake and crept along the bank.

The ice creaked beneath their boots as they huddled together. Hoofbeats thundered past above, sending chips of stone skittering down on to the lake. Suddenly, an animal's scream of terror set Tom's nerves thrumming. With a crash, a skinny calf landed on the ice. It scrambled up, its eyes rolling and its feet skidding in all directions as it tried to balance.

Tom heard an ominous snapping sound and gasped as zigzag cracks shot across the ice towards him from where the calf struggled. One of the creature's hooves crashed through the thin crust of ice. Black water oozed up around it as more cracks followed. The calf snorted and bucked in terror, making its way towards Tom and Elenna, the ice giving way beneath its weight. *It's going down – and so are we!* Tom realised. *No!* He shoved Elenna hard, sending her skidding away from the breaking ice. A second later the ice splintered beneath Tom's feet with a crash. He cried out as he fell.

Knife-sharp cold shocked Tom

to the core, making all his muscles clench and snatching the air from his lungs. *Don't panic!* he told himself. *Breathe!* He forced his trembling body to relax and took a shuddering gasp of air. With legs already as numb as blocks of wood, he trod water, and made a grab for the terrified calf. But as his cold, stiff fingers gripped the animal's hide, the calf thrashed, breaking from his grasp. With one last, desperate look of terror, the calf sank into the freezing depths.

Through chattering teeth, Tom took a final breath and dived. As the water closed around his skull like an icy clamp, he knew he was being a fool – but he couldn't watch an innocent creature drown. He kicked his numb legs and reached down after the sinking animal.

The light around him faded and his lungs started to throb. The cold felt like thousands of needles piercing him to the core, but he kicked deeper, arms outstretched. Finally, his fingers tangled in shaggy hair. *Got it!* Tom wrapped one arm around the struggling creature's neck and kicked for the surface.

Tom's sodden clothes and the heavy calf weighed him down. The pressure in his lungs became almost unbearable but he clamped his teeth shut against the deadly urge to breathe. Looking up, he could see only faint moonlight, shining though unbroken ice. Panic jolted through him. *Where's the hole?*

Tom's lungs shuddered for breath.

Cold stabbed him anew with every stroke and his sluggish limbs barely seemed to move. *I'm trapped! I'm going to drown!* As his vision began to fade, and numbness spread through his body, he thought of the golden ring in his pocket... *The only proof of Angelo's death is going to drown here, with me*, he realised. *I'm going to die and leave the kingdom in the hands of an evil tyrant... I've failed Avantia!*

1

4

RESCUE

Tom reached up, his freezing fingers stubbing weakly against the pale ice. He made a fist, trying to break through, but his arm had no strength. Blackness began to close in around the edges of his vision. His lungs screamed for air. Then, suddenly, the ice above him cracked and bright rays of moonlight slanted through. A hand grabbed his wrist. More hands followed, gripping his arms and shoulders, heaving him up out of the icy water.

Tom gasped and shuddered, trying to gulp air through his chattering teeth. He felt the calf lifted from his hold. Elenna's worried face swam into focus, then those of hooded and bearded men, speaking in urgent voices. *Cowherds*, he realised. He tried to speak, but his body shook so violently he could only grunt. Strong hands gripped his shoulders once more, tugging him across the ice towards safety.

Tom's fingers burned with welcome pain as he held them before the campfire. *At least I don't have frostbite!* The rising sun cast a rosy glow over the icy peaks all around him as the stars vanished one by one in the pale dawn sky. Wrapped in thick woollen blankets and with a belly full of soup, Tom finally felt warm. The rescued calf, pressed close against him, shifted and nuzzled his leg. Since her rescue, she hadn't left his side.

"You've made a friend for life there, boy," said Henrik, the lead cowherd, tipping his head towards the calf. "I'm glad to see you're starting to thaw. I was worried you'd

not make it when we pulled you
from the ice. I owe you my thanks for
rescuing her. And an apology. When
I blew the warning horn, it spooked

the calf on to the ice. Turns out it was a false alarm."

"False alarm for what?" Elenna asked.

"Life in these parts is perilous," Henrik said. "We must bring the herd into the mountains to graze, but, up here, Torka patrols the sky."

"Torka... A flying Beast?" said Tom.

"Aye," said the cowherd. "She's got a taste for our cattle. But she's not fussy. She'll take a person too – even a child if she can get them."

Tom sensed Elenna staring at him. He knew what she was thinking, because his own mind was troubled by the same dilemma. *How can we leave these people to be plagued by a Beast?*

"We're travelling to Avantia," Tom said, "but we'll stay and deal with Torka first."

Henrik regarded Tom with a puzzled frown. One of his men let out a stifled laugh, and Tom looked up to see the cowherds exchanging doubtful smiles and nudging each other. Hot blood rushed to his face. *I must look little more than a half-drowned child*, he thought. But then cold, hard reality washed over him. *Without my powers, maybe that's all I am...*

"After almost getting you killed, there's no way I'm letting you face

Torka," Henrik said. "My lad Ash over there will see you safely over the mountains." He nodded towards a tall boy with fair hair and wind-reddened cheeks, wearing a dark cloak and scarf. "Ash is sure-footed and quick. He'll see you right. I couldn't forgive myself if we left you to face the same fate as those two poor women."

"What women?" Tom asked.

Henrik let out a heavy sigh, his expression turning suddenly grave. "An older lady and her daughter moved into an abandoned hut in the next valley," he said. "Torka took them just a few days ago."

Tom frowned. "Well, in that case

we definitely can't—" A sudden horn blast drowned out Tom's words.

"Torka!" Henrik cried. All around him, the cowherds broke into action, shouldering packs or tugging pouches from their belts.

Nudging the calf away, Tom leaped up.

Elenna was at his side in an instant. "Get behind us!" she shouted to the cowherds, fitting an arrow to her bow and aiming it out into the pale grey dawn.

Henrik's mouth dropped open. "It's you young folks who should take cover," he said. "We've our own way of dealing with the Beast."

Tom turned back to see several of

Henrik's cowherds hurriedly tipping powders from pouches into clay tubes tied to sticks while others were already leading the snorting cattle further down the mountainside. Soft pops and fizzes erupted from the mixed powders, and Tom caught a whiff like rotting eggs or pond slime.

"Ash, you set off the flares," Henrik told his son. "Catch up with us once the Beast has gone." Ash nodded, and lit a long taper from the campfire, just as another mighty horn blast echoed through the mountains.

"We'll stay with Ash," Tom told Henrik. "We'll defend him if the Beast swoops."

Henrik looked as if he might be

about to argue, but then he took in Elenna's bow, and Tom's sword and shield, and nodded. "Right you are," he said, "but stay safe!" Then the big man turned to hurry down the mountain path after his herd.

Ash crouched low to the ground, the tip of his smouldering taper glowing, and his breath hanging in the cold air. A small forest of sticks with smoking clay pipes stuck up from the snow beside him. "Stay back," the boy told Tom and Elenna. They watched as Ash touched the red tip of his splint to a fuse sticking from the base of one of the pipes. Immediately, the fuse started to sizzle. A moment later, the clay pipe whooshed up into the air and exploded in a starburst of golden sparks. A resounding *boom* followed, so loud Tom felt it in his lungs. Ash worked quickly, lighting each fuse. Another missile followed the first, then another. Soon the whole sky seemed to blaze with sparks and a sound like cannon fire echoed through the mountains.

Tom and Elenna stood back to back, scanning the horizon, their weapons raised. Suddenly, a huge dark and bloated form with broad, scaled wings swooped from over a snowy peak.

"There!" Tom cried, pointing as Elenna sprang to his side.

The Beast flapped down the mountainside, swooping low through Ash's flares. A sinuous reptilian tail streamed behind her but, instead of a dragon's head, she had three long, feathered necks, each bearing the bald, wrinkled skull of a carrion-eating bird. Six eyes shone with a ravenous light as they fixed on the fleeing cattle, and three, huge pelican-like beaks gaped wide enough to swallow an animal whole.

5

TORKA SWOOPS

Tom crouched, sword raised, as Torka banked steeply, her massive dragon body filling the sky, and her six bright eyes fixed on the herd of cattle further down the mountain path.

Two of Ash's flares whizzed past the dragon-bird, exploding with flashes and thunderous bangs.

Panicked snorts and screams from the cows mingled with urgent cries from the cowherds.

As Torka drew closer, the terrible stench of rotting meat hit Tom, making his stomach heave. The Beast's eyes seemed to glow like burning coals, and strands of putrid flesh hung from the saw-like, bloodstained edges of her open beaks.

Elenna let an arrow fly. *Thwack!* It struck the Beast's scaled hide but ricocheted off. Elenna quickly fired another shot. *THUNK!* This one lodged in Torka's wing. The Beast screamed with fury, blasting them with the vile reek of death and decay.

Then, fixing Elenna with all three pairs of livid eyes, she angled her long necks downwards and dived.

"Get down!" Tom cried. As Elenna threw herself to the ground, Tom leaped before her, sword raised at the speeding Beast. With a screech of fury, the Beast sent one of her three beaks snapping towards him. Tom drew back his sword... *CRACK!* The flat of his blade smacked hard across Torka's bill, knocking it aside, and sending a jolt of agony up Tom's arm.

Shrieking with rage, Torka banked upwards out of Tom's reach. Elenna leaped to her feet, ready to send an arrow after the dragon-bird – but at the same moment, one of Ash's flares exploded right before them, blinding them with searing light. Tom heard the sweep of giant wings overhead, closely followed by the hideous, panicked scream of an animal. When his eyes focused, he turned to see

Torka surging into the sky with a fat cow struggling in one of her giant beaks. Elenna let her arrow fly, but already the Beast had climbed out of range. The shaft clattered harmlessly to the ground as Torka disappeared

over a snowy peak and into the fiery light of the rising sun.

"Where will she take the cow?" Tom asked Ash, sheathing his sword, ready to run.

"Over that peak," the boy said, pointing the way the Beast had gone. "You'll see a hut there in a shallow valley. The Beast's lair is on the other side, roughly above the hut. But you can't go there. Torka will eat you just like she ate the woman and her girl."

"You saw her eat them?" Elenna asked, her eyes wide with horror.

Ash shook his head. "No," he said. "But Torka left claw prints everywhere. We had warned the women to leave, but they wouldn't. They were kind to us. They even made healing ointments for when the cattle got injured. But now they're gone."

"If you didn't see them die, there's a chance they're still alive," Elenna said. "We should check the valley, and Torka's lair."

Tom nodded. And though his stomach churned at the thought of facing the three-headed Beast without his Golden Armour, he knew they couldn't leave her free to pick off cattle and travellers one by one. "Let's go!" he said.

Ash shook his head, his eyes wide. "You two are crazy!" he said.

Then he let out a sigh. "You'd better take these." He crossed to where a handful of unspent flares still poked up from the snow, and plucked them from the ground. "If the Beast attacks, these might give you a

chance to escape," he said, handing them to Tom.

"Thank you," Tom said, shoving the sticks through his belt.

Ash wished them luck, then turned to follow the path of churned snow after the herd, while Tom and Elenna started the steep climb towards the peak. As they scrambled up the snowy slope, Tom couldn't help thinking how little Ash's flares had seemed to deter the Beast. He swallowed hard. *But apart from my sword and Elenna's bow, that's all we have...*

The sun rose steadily as Tom and Elenna climbed, turning the sky a watery blue, but the air seemed only to grow colder. Soon every breath burned in Tom's lungs and his face and even his teeth ached. Several times, he lost his footing and slipped on the jagged ice, scraping his hands until his frozen skin looked red-raw.

At last, Tom and Elenna stepped up on to the top of the mountain range. The bitter wind slammed into them, making them stagger. Tom shielded his eyes and looked down into the valley below. Another glacial lake, gleaming like polished silver in the sun, covered most of the valley floor. On the nearest shore, close to the foot of the slope, sat the lonely ruins of a two-storey wooden

cottage. A pile of firewood stood at
the front of the dwelling, but the
door hung open, half torn off its
hinges. Tom scanned the ridges of
ice and rock on the far side of the

valley, looking for any sign of the Beast or its lair, but the snow seemed undisturbed. He was just about to suggest they set off again, when he heard a faint cry – high-pitched and female – carried on the icy wind.

"Listen," he hissed. Elenna tipped her head.

"Help! Please! Help!" the muffled voice cried.

"It's coming from down there," Elenna said, pointing towards the hut.

"The women did survive!" Tom exclaimed, striking off down the rocky slope. "We have to help them!"

TRAPPED

Tom and Elenna half scrambled, half ran down the steep mountainside towards the hut. As they drew closer, Tom could see that part of the roof had collapsed, bringing one of the walls down with it. The muffled cries they heard seemed to be coming from beneath the fallen beams.

"You take that end," Tom told Elenna, pointing to the topmost log. "Lift on three. One...two...three!"

They heaved the wooden beam up together, both staggering under its weight as they carried it aside.

"HELP! I'm down here!" the voice cried, more urgently than ever. Tom frowned. The muffled tones sounded vaguely familiar.

"Stay where you are," he called back. "We'll get you free."

After a pause, Tom heard an exasperated groan from beneath the wreckage of the hut. "Please tell me that isn't Tom and Elenna," the voice said wearily.

"Petra!" Elenna cried. She

clenched her teeth, her face turning red. "What are you doing here?"

Tom felt his frown deepen. *How is that possible?* Petra was the witch Kapra's daughter, and they hadn't seen her for months.

"I could ask you the same thing!" Petra grumbled. "You'd think you were my own personal fan club, the way you follow me around."

"We could just leave now, you know!" Elenna said.

Tom put a hand on her arm. "Let's just get Petra out of there," he said gently. "We can find out what she knows about the false Angelo, and what her mother's up to, afterwards."

"Fine," Elenna said, scowling. Together they shifted all the logs until they had cleared a space on the hut's wooden floor, exposing a hinged trapdoor. Tom pulled it open. Petra squinted up at him, her face covered in filth and her hair like a tangled rat's nest, complete with cobwebs. As Tom offered her his hand, he felt the young witch shiver. Her fingers were icy cold. *She must have been down here for days*, Tom realised. *Lucky we came when we did, or she would have perished.*

Petra clambered out of the cellar and hugged her grimy cloak about her, blinking in the sunlight. She looked thinner than Tom

remembered, but uninjured.

"Right," Elenna said, rounding

on the witch, "you'd better tell us everything you know about your mother's latest evil plans. Now!"

Petra gawked at her, then frowned. "I don't know what you're talking about," she said. She sounded genuinely upset. "My mother's dead!"

Elenna rolled her eyes. "Yeah, right," she said. "Well, she definitely wasn't a few days ago when she rode into Avantia with a bunch of barbarians and stole King Hugo's throne."

Petra's brown eyes opened wide, then she let out a whoop of joy.

Tom felt a wave of frustration. "Didn't you hear what Elenna just said?" he asked. "Your mother's helped an imposter usurp King Hugo!"

Petra shook her head, still grinning. "Yes… It's just that I thought she was dead. When Torka attacked, Mother was outside. I assumed she was killed, but now you're saying she's alive! Well, that's brilliant news."

Tom let out a heavy sigh. "It does rather mean she abandoned you to the Beast though, doesn't it?" he said. "I hope Angelo promised her something pretty special as a reward."

Petra hitched her chin. "I'm sure she had a good reason for leaving when she did," she said.

"Clearly," Elenna said, "she was more interested in stirring up trouble in Avantia than saving her own daughter. And what were the pair of you doing here in the Wildlands anyway?"

Petra sniffed. "If you must know, we came here for a break – to get away from prejudice," she said, fixing Elenna with a glare.

"If you seriously expect us to believe that, you're—" Elenna stopped. Petra's eyes had opened wide, staring at something behind Tom and Elenna. "What?" Elenna said.

"Get down!" Petra screamed, just

as the sound of wingbeats filled
the air. A huge shadow blocked out
the sunlight, bringing with it the
stench of rotting meat. Tom drew his
sword and spun to see Torka bearing
down on them. One of the Beast's

long feathered necks stretched out towards Elenna. Before Tom could do a thing, the bill snapped closed over his friend, and snatched her up.

"No!" Tom cried, racing after the dragon-bird as she flapped away.

"Help!" Elenna screamed. But Torka climbed quickly, carrying her high into the wintry sky.

THE THREE-HEADED MENACE

Tom raced over the valley floor, keeping Torka and Elenna right above him. The look of terror in Elenna's eyes filled him with horror and rage. *But without even a bow and arrow, how can I help her?* Then, with a sudden flash of hope, Tom remembered the flares he carried. *I need to get to higher ground!*

Tom reached the valley side and started to scramble upwards as fast as he could. He could hear Petra behind him, panting to keep up. Glancing skywards, he saw Elenna dangling from Torka's cruel, bloodstained beak, her face contorted with agony. Though his legs burned and the breath rasped in his throat, he forced himself to climb even faster.

As soon as Tom reached the peak, he snatched a flare from his belt and shook his flint and tinder from their pouch. His fingers felt clumsy, and frustration burned inside him as he hurried to strike a flame. Three pairs of cruel amber eyes gazed down at him, full of gloating joy.

"Let...me," Petra gasped, arriving at his side. She focussed her eyes on the flare in Tom's hand, then muttered a strange word. The fuse sizzled into life.

"Thank you!" Tom said. He drew back his arm and threw the explosive hard and high, aiming straight at the dragon-bird. The flare arced through the air, peaking far too low. *No!* Tom growled with frustration as the missile sailed past Torka, exploding with a *boom* above the frozen lake.

Petra shot Tom a puzzled frown. "What's wrong with your arm?" she asked. "Even for you, that throw was kind of weak."

Tom sighed, too filled with horror and worry to be angry. "Your mother melted my Golden Armour, that's what," he said.

Petra shook her head. "No...she wouldn't... Would she?"

Already pulling another flare from his belt, Tom ignored the question and held the explosive out towards her. Petra gaped at him for a moment, but then quickly focussed on the fuse.

Fixing his gaze on the Beast's scaled chest, where he guessed its heart must be, Tom took a deep and shuddering breath. Drawing on all his rage, summoning every bit of power he had, he threw the flare. It fizzed and sizzled through the air, up towards the Beast. *BOOM!* The firework still didn't reach its mark. Instead, it exploded right beside one

of the Beast's hideous bald heads. Two huge beaks opened at once, letting out twin screeches of rage.

The central beak, which held Elenna, flicked upwards and opened too, tossing her into the sky. Tom's heart clenched. Elenna let out a cry of terror as she flew through the air, then a yelp of pain as the Beast caught her again in a saw-toothed bill.

"Tom, you really need to hit that thing this time," Petra said, her eyes wide and serious as she handed him a lit flare. "Otherwise, I think Elenna's dead."

Panic squeezed Tom's chest so hard he could barely breathe. He

flung the explosive wildly at the
dragon-bird. The flare burst into
a spray of golden sparks beneath
Torka's scaled belly. Again, the
Beast let out furious screeches, and
tossed Elenna. But this time Elenna
didn't cry out at all as the Beast's
bill snapped shut around her.
Instead, she slumped like a rag doll,
her eyes closed.

*This isn't working! I'm not strong
enough!* Tom swallowed hard, trying
to stop his hands shaking and
his heart hammering with dread.
Sickness churned in his stomach
and he could taste bile in his throat.
Without his magical chainmail
for strength of heart, adrenaline

coursed through his veins like poison, making him jittery and faint.

"Come on, Tom," Petra said urgently. "You can do this!" She grabbed the last few flares from his belt and held one before her eyes until it started to smoke.

Tom closed his eyes for a moment, and clenched his fists, thinking hard. *I need a new plan. If I can't reach the Beast, I'll have to bring her to me.* He took the lit flare from Petra, who stepped back with a firm nod.

But this time, Tom didn't throw the explosive. Instead, he looked up at the Beast hanging in the air above him, a dark inkblot of evil. Fear surged through him as three pairs of cruel eyes rimmed with red fleshy wrinkles met his own. But he swallowed hard and started to wave the flare in his hand.

"Scared, are you, you outsized, bird-brained lizard?" Tom shouted. The Beast's eyes narrowed, and Tom heard a chorus of rumbling growls come from deep in its feathered throats. "Are you too afraid to face a boy without even a bow and arrow?" Tom shouted. "A little bang from a firework and you're too chicken to fight?"

The Beast lowered her vulture-like heads, threw back her dragon wings and with two wild screams of rage, she dived.

Tom held his ground as Torka plunged towards him, two of her vast beaks gaping wide. Elenna hung limply in the third, her face deathly pale. Tom's gut tightened with fear. *I hope I'm not too late!* As the Beast drew closer, the reek of rotten flesh made him gasp. He focussed on the Beast's nearest head, staring past Torka's bloody teeth deep into the dark and putrid cavern of her throat. As the Beast's eyes flashed with victory and her colossal beak spread wider, right above Tom, he forced himself to wait just a heartbeat more. Then finally, at the last possible moment, he drew back his arm and lobbed his explosive right into Torka's mouth.

As Tom threw himself sideways into the snow, the Beast's bill snapped shut right where he had just

been standing.

Tom heard a muffled *BOOM!*

"Nice shot!" Petra cried.

Tom rolled into a crouch and looked up. Torka writhed in the air above him, flapping her wings

crazily and shaking her bald heads.
Elenna groaned, her limbs jerking as
the Beast jolted her about. Two sets
of the Beast's eyes rolled in pain, but
the third set had turned milky white.
As Tom watched, the clouded eyes

fell closed, and the Beast's injured head slumped downwards to dangle limply on its neck.

Tom felt a rush of hope as the Beast tumbled towards the mountainside. But then Torka opened her two remaining beaks in a screech of defiance, releasing Elenna from her grip.

Hot terror knifed through Tom's gut as Elenna plummeted. *She'll be killed!* But before Elenna could hit the rocks, Petra leaped to Tom's side, hands outstretched. A blue web of light unfurled from her open fingers and closed about Elenna like a net, slowing her fall. Petra started to reel the net in, tugging Elenna towards

her while the Beast crashed down on
to the slope in a tangle of feathers,
claws and scales.

Tom drew his sword and raced over
the icy rock towards Torka. *I have to
finish this while she's down!* But as

he approached the fallen Beast, four of her glowing eyes flicked open, and she kicked out at him with a taloned foot.

Tom tried to dodge, but the clawed foot caught his shoulder, smashing the breath from his body, and sending him tumbling down the slope...

1

FIRE IN THE SKY

Sharp rock and jagged ice pummelled and stabbed at Tom as he rolled down the mountainside. Finally, he came to rest on a ledge, gasping for breath, every part of his body screaming with pain. He scrambled to his feet and drew his sword just as a shadow fell over him and the putrid stench of rot hit him like a fist.

"SQUAWK!" Torka's open beak snapped towards him. Tom swung his sword and batted it away, but another bill jabbed for his chest. Before he could block, the tip hit him hard in the ribs, catapulting him backwards. As he hit the slope once more, his sword flew from his grip and his head cracked against a rock. He tumbled over and over, picking up speed, pain and dizziness filling his senses.

"Oof!" He hit the valley floor and skidded to a stop. Shaking his head to clear his vision, Tom found himself right on the edge of the frozen lake. He shuddered, remembering his recent brush with a watery grave. But then an idea came to him.

Tom turned to see the dragon-bird flapping clumsily towards him, one neck dangling, and one of her wings hanging crookedly at her side. *She must have been injured when she fell!* Tom realised. *This might just work!* Trying not to think of the dark waters waiting to claim him below, Tom stepped on to the frozen lake and started to run.

Glancing back, he saw Torka following him, moving quickly as her clawed feet gripped the ice. But with the treads of his boots soon filling with snow, Tom's own feet slid apart and he fell. He hit the

ice and scrambled up, his hands
stinging, and glanced back to see
the Beast gaining on him, cracks
spreading out from beneath her
huge taloned feet.

"Tom, you fool! Get off the ice!"
Petra screamed. Tom looked back
to see her kneeling beside Elenna,
propping her up with one arm. "It's
going to break!"

That's what I'm counting on!
Tom thought. He pushed himself
to his feet, and took off again, half
running, half sliding, further out on
to the ice. He could hear the Beast's
heavy steps right behind him now,
and the cracking of the ice beneath
her was loud in his ears. But still,

the frozen surface didn't give.

BOOF! A scaled wing slammed
into Tom, sending him spinning
through the air. He hit the ice

shoulder first, then skidded. When he finally came to a stop, winded, he rolled on to his back to see Torka prowling towards him over the frozen lake. Her injured wing dragged on the ice and one head lolled groggily. But the Beast's four remaining eyes glared at him with a hatred so intense that even without his red jewel, it filled him with terror and awe.

More cracks spread across the ice with echoing pings and snaps, but still the Beast edged closer to him, the light of victory kindling in her eyes. Tom watched with helpless dread. *The ice on this lake must be thicker!* he realised. *And now I've nowhere to go. I'm going to die, which means King*

Hugo will never know the truth about his brother!

"Tom!" Petra called. Her voice sounded closer now, and Tom looked up to see her and Elenna standing on the shore of the lake. The sight of his dear friend on her feet gave him new hope and strength. And, as he watched, Petra drew back her arm and threw something glittering towards him. *A lit flare!* Tom realised, as it arced through the air. The explosive landed on the ice and skidded on, coming to rest right between him and the Beast.

Torka let out two squawks of fury as her eyes fell on the smoking flare. She stopped in her tracks and drew back her feathered necks, as if afraid. Tom knew Petra had given him the chance he needed – a slim one, but he wasn't about to let it pass. He scrambled forward and snatched the explosive up. Looking at the vast Beast, he knew one flare wouldn't be enough to defeat it. *Unless...*

Tom threw the flare on to the ice, directly beneath the Beast's clawed feet, then scrambled backwards as fast as he could. With a screech of fury, a long, feathered neck darted towards him, and the Beast's bill gaped wide, ready to snap shut...

BOOM! A flare of light blinded Tom. His ears rang. As the echoing

explosion died away the sound of splitting ice filled the air, along with a furious screeching and the whip-like slap of giant wings.

Tom blinked and focussed his eyes

to see Torka beating her wings and clawing at the ice as her massive, scaled body began to sink through the fractured surface. He pushed himself away from the spreading cracks as the Beast fell further, her wings useless against the freezing water. She let out a series of harsh, panicked squawks. Finally, only two feathered heads remained above the surface. Torka shot Tom one last venomous look, then her heads sank too. He watched the bubbling pool of water for any signs of life, but nothing emerged. The Beast was gone for ever.

He heard a whoop and looked across the lake to see Petra

punching the air.

Shakily, he pulled himself to his feet, and giving the huge dark hole in the ice a wide berth, walked carefully back to shore.

As soon as he reached firm, dry land, Elenna rushed towards him. He felt all his aches and pains recede at the sight of her safe and well.

"I can't believe you're alive!" Elenna said, folding him in a quick hug.

Behind Elenna, Petra smirked. "He wouldn't be if it weren't for me," she said. "What would Avantia's favourite hero do without Petra the witch, huh?"

Tom couldn't help but grin. "I supposed that flare did come in kind of handy..." he said.

Elenna smiled too. "I guess that just about pays us back for digging you out of that cellar then, hey?" she said.

As Petra and Elenna exchanged jokey scowls, Tom's eyes fell on the wreckage of the cabin behind them. They still hadn't worked out why Kapra had abandoned Petra to a frozen death out here in the mountains. What was it that had lured her to Avantia with the false king?

And what terrible tyranny reigns at this very moment?

"We're not done yet," Tom said. "We need to get back to Avantia – and fast."

"Can't we have a little rest first?" said Petra. "I mean, just to pat ourselves on the back for a job well done."

"No!" said Tom and Elenna together, before Tom added: "This Quest isn't over. And while there's blood in my veins, I won't stop fighting."

"How did I know you'd say that?" muttered Petra.

"Come on," said Tom, pointing towards a ridge rising above the lake to the south. "It's that way."

Petra looked at him doubtfully,

then grinned. "It just so happens, I might know a quicker way…"

THE END

CONGRATULATIONS, YOU HAVE COMPLETED THIS QUEST!

At the end of each chapter you were awarded a special gold coin.
The QUEST in this book was worth an amazing 8 coins.

Look at the Beast Quest totem picture opposite to see how far you've come in your journey to become

MASTER OF THE BEASTS.

The more books you read, the more coins you will collect!

Do you want your own
Beast Quest Totem?

1. Cut out and collect the coin below
2. Go to the Beast Quest website
3. Download and print out your totem
4. Add your coin to the totem

www.beastquest.co.uk

READ THE BOOKS, COLLECT THE COINS!
EARN COINS FOR EVERY CHAPTER YOU READ!

550+ COINS
MASTER OF
THE BEASTS

410 COINS
HERO

350 COINS
WARRIOR

230 COINS
KNIGHT

180 COINS
SQUIRE

44 COINS
PAGE

8 COINS
APPRENTICE

READ ALL THE BOOKS IN SERIES 23:
THE SHATTERED KINGDOM!

QUERZOL
THE SWAMP MONSTER

KROTAX
THE TUSKED DESTROYER

TORKA
THE SKY SNATCHER

XERKAN
THE SHAPE STEALER

BeastQuest
NEW BLOOD
ADAM BLADE

Meet three new heroes with the power to tame the Beasts!

Amy, Charlie and Sam – three children
from our world – are about to discover the
powerful legacy that binds them together.

They are descendants of the *Guardians of
Avantia*, an elite group of heroes trained by
Tom himself.

Now the time has come for a new generation
to unlock the power of the Beasts and
fulfil their destiny.

*Read on for a sneak peek at how the
Guardians first left Avantia by magic…*

Karita of Banquise gazed in awe at Tom, Avantia's mighty, bearded Master of the Beasts.

Under his leadership, she and her companions would today face their greatest challenge.

Tom pointed towards the brooding Gorgonian castle. "We must recover the chest of Beast Eggs Malvel stole," he reminded them. His fierce blue eyes moved from Karita to the others. Dell of Stonewin, whose bloodline connected him to Beasts of Fire; Fern of Errinel, linked to Storm Beasts; Gustus of Colton, bonded with Water Beasts.

"Malvel will be expecting an attack," Tom said. "His power is lessened, but he is still formidable." His eyes locked on Karita. "Stealth will be our greatest ally."

Karita felt as though her whole life had been a preparation for this moment. Countless hours spent studying the ancient tomes, day after day of gruelling combat training, months learning how to influence the will of Stealth Beasts and control the powers that filled the Arcane Band at her wrist.

But was she ready?

She gazed into Tom's face, and her doubts faded.

Yes!

A low rumble came from the

castle. Flashes of green lightning shot from the clouds as a swarm of screeching creatures erupted from the battlements.

Karita shuddered as Malvel's hideous minions streaked through the sky. They were man-sized, with white hides, limbs tipped with hooked claws and gaping jaws lined with sharp teeth. Their leathery wings cracked like whips.

"Karrakhs!" muttered Tom. "Karita – go!"

She nodded and slipped away behind jagged rocks. She turned to see the swarm of foul creatures engulf her companions. Tom's sword flashed. Howls rang out from the Karrakhs. The Guardians were using

their Arcane Bands to form weapons
that spun and slashed!

Karita raced for the castle, keeping
low behind the ridge of rocks.
Reaching the walls, she climbed up
a gnarled vine and found a narrow
window to crawl through. She
looked back again. Tom and the
Guardians had battled their way
through the castle gates.

Well fought!

She dropped into a room and crept
to the door. Torches burned in the
corridor, casting shadows. The castle
was silent, but Karita felt a growing
dread as she slipped along the walls.

She knew where the chest of Beast
eggs was hidden. But would Malvel
allow her to get to them?

She came to a circular room, and saw the chest standing by the wall. Her heart hammering, Karita opened the lid and gazed down at the eggs. They were different sizes, shapes and colours. One slipped from the pile and she caught it in her gloved hand. It was pale blue, about the size of a goose egg. Acting on instinct, she slipped it inside her breastplate.

Crash!

She spun around. Malvel stood against the room's closed door.

"Did you really think you could enter my domain unseen?" he snarled, a green glow igniting in his palm. His voice was weaker than she'd imagined. "I *wanted* you to come here. After all, only a Guardian can hatch a Beast Egg."

Karita swallowed hard, seeking a
way to escape.

"You and your friends will hatch
these Beasts and I will drink in their
power," growled the wizard. "I will
become mighty again and Avantia
will bow before me!"

"I'm not afraid of you!" Karita
shouted.

A ball of green fire exploded from
Malvel's hand. Karita dived aside,
seared by the heat.

She leaped up, thrusting her right
arm towards the wizard. The Arcane
Band began to form a weapon, but
another blast of fire sent her sliding
across the floor.

Malvel loomed over her, both hands

burning green. Before he could strike, the door burst open and Tom and the Guardians rushed into the room.

"No!" roared Malvel. "Where are my Karrakhs?"

"Defeated!" shouted Tom, whirling his sword to deflect Malvel's green flames. "Guardians! Take the eggs!"

Fern dived for the chest, but a blast from the wizard knocked her over.

"The eggs are mine!" howled Malvel. He traced a large circle of fire in the air. There was a blast of hot wind as the flaming hoop crackled and spat.

Malvel snatched up the chest and turned to the heart of the fiery circle.

"He's opened a portal!" shouted

Tom. "Stop him!"

Gustus ran at the wizard and wrested the chest from his grip. Roaring in anger, Malvel launched a fireball, but Fern managed to shove Gustus out of its path. But the force of her push knocked Gustus into the portal. With a stifled cry, he and the chest of eggs were gone.

"No!" Fern shouted, diving in after him. With a shout, Dell ran after her.

"Wait!" shouted Tom.

"It's our duty to protect the eggs!" Dell called back as he disappeared into the swirling portal.

Malvel sprang forward, but Tom bounded in front of him, holding him back with his spinning blade as the wizard hurled magical fireballs.

Karita saw the walls of the portal writhing and distorting. Malvel's fireballs were making it unstable. At any moment it might vanish!

Tom was knocked back by a torrent of green fire as the wizard turned and leaped into the portal. Karita flung herself after him.

"No! Karita!" The last thing she heard was Tom's voice. "The portal is in flux! You could be sent anywhere!"

And then there was nothing but a rushing wind and howling darkness, as she plunged into the unknown.

Look out for
Beast Quest: New Blood
to find out what happens next!

Don't miss the next exciting
Beast Quest Special:

SCALAMANX
THE FIERY FURY

OUT NOW!

The epic adventure is brought
to life on **Xbox One** and **PS4**
for the first time ever!

www.maximumgames.com   www.beast-quest.com